CONTACT INITIATIVE

To The Stars & Sky's the Limit

Leah Lore

Through the Rift Publishing

Visit: Linktr.ee/LeahLore

ISBN: 978-1-966638-01-8

For everyone out there searching for your place.
May you reach the stars.

Contents

To the Stars

Stars

Through the Rift Publishing

One

"What are you doing here, Paige?"

The Captain frowned down at me with narrowed blue eyes. The pilot's pin on his lapel glinted even in the diffuse sunlight that filtered into the large hangar through dirty skylights. The metallic wings against the navy blue flight suit reminded me of the fighter jets that flew by my window every evening.

"Cadet Paige, reporting for duty, sir!"

His eyes widened as he took in my blue pajamas-turned-flight suit, noting the name I scribbled onto the chest pocket with permanent marker. I was proud of my makeshift uniform. I thought he would be too. After all, he was the one who said he couldn't find a flight suit small enough to fit a seven-year-old.

"Does your mother know you're here?" His concerned expression had me doubting myself. Maybe this *wasn't* such a good idea.

"Well . . . No."

I deflated along with his exasperated sigh. "She'll be worried sick. You need to go home." I frowned as he looked around for someone. "Cadet Cassowary?"

"Yes, Captain?" A thin girl stepped forward. She had glasses and blue streaks running through her blonde hair. I was so captivated by the colors, I momentarily forgot I was being banished.

"Are you familiar with the Officers' Quarters?"

"Somewhat, sir."

"Please escort my daughter home. We live in 16C."

"Daddy, I wanna help!"

He kneeled down in front of me, bringing his face level with mine. His serious expression etched into my mind.

"You aren't old enough to be a cadet yet."

"But Daddy!" I stomped my dress-up army boot, tiny compared to his. "I wanna learn!"

"You will, sweetheart. When you're older."

"But you do it now!" I whined.

"Yes." A smile crinkled the edges of his cheeks, making him look much more like the man who played starships with me before bedtime. "Because I'm already older. Now get going."

"Come on, kiddo. Let's get you home, okay?" Cadet Cassowary held out her hand to me. I eyed the blue-haired girl suspiciously. "My name's Amara. You can ask me questions about being a cadet, if you want."

I brightened at that and grabbed her hand. I smiled up at my new friend.

"Okay," I said with a smile. "But only 'cause your hair is really pretty."

"Come on, Daddy!" I whined, grabbing his hand and pulling him toward the window at the end of the hallway. "We're going to miss the stars!"

"I don't think the stars are going anywhere, Paige," he said tiredly. He was always tired when he came home.

"That's what I said," my mother called from the antique leather couch in the living room, "but she wouldn't listen!"

"Seems like she's not listening a lot these days," my father grumbled, but he let me pull him out to the fire escape.

We waited there for my mother to join us—my father helping her out through the window—before climbing up to the roof. Two lawn chairs and a picnic blanket were still set up from the previous blackout last week. I jumped up and down waiting for my mom to sit in one of the chairs before crawling into her lap.

"How did she get away from you today?" my father asked.

"Honestly, I have no idea." My mother put her arms around me while I twisted around to better see the sky. "One minute she was napping, the next minute that cadet with the blue hair was knocking on the door."

"That was Amara. She's my new friend!" I said, proudly. "I want pretty hair like hers."

"We'll see, sweetheart." Mom smiled at me before turning back to dad. "You're home late. Is everything okay? The jets sounded closer this evening."

Dad sighed and rubbed the back of his neck. "They were. One of the other Civs caught us off guard. I don't know how they did it, but they snuck past our outer defenses. Luckily, some of our newer pilots were in a training exercise and able to hold them off until reinforcements arrived."

"Newer pilots?" Mom's eyebrows raised. "You put sixteen-year-olds in combat?"

"*I* didn't put them anywhere."

"Kids shouldn't have to kill—"

"Daddy, what's that star?" I interrupted. We were up here to learn about stars, not *talk* with each other. The blackouts were the only times it was dark enough to see them. I didn't want to waste any more time. Dad took a deep breath before looking where I pointed.

"You already know that one, don't you?" he asked with a smile.

"Yeah, that's Polaris. I was just testing you."

"Oh, you were?" He laughed. "Okay, smarty-pants. What's the name of that star over there?"

We quizzed each other on the stars until my eyelids started to get heavy.

"Is it bedtime, sweetheart?" Mom asked.

"No, I wanna go up there!"

"Up there?" Dad asked, glancing at the sky. "To the stars?"

"To the stars!" I yelled the words like a battle call, fighting the fatigue trying to overcome me. Mom and Dad shushed me, but we all erupted into giggles.

"Quiet, you'll wake the neighbors," Dad said.

"To the stars!" I whispered, still laughing.

"To the stars, sugar plum," Mom whisper-laughed along with me. We both looked at Dad, who rolled his eyes, but smiled.

"To the stars."

When I could no longer keep my eyes open, I snuggled against my mom. She ran her fingers through my hair and I drifted to sleep under the murmur of their quiet conversation.

Two

"What are you doing here Paige?"

"Cadet Pearson, reporting for duty, sir!"

I held my salute until the Captain released me. Then I stood at ease—my head high, my back straight, my eyes trained in the distance ten degrees above the horizon and my expression serious. Exactly how he showed me.

"You aren't a cadet." The Captain's voice was weary. I risked a glance at his face. His hair—once as black as mine—was now peppered with gray and the electric blue eyes that I inherited were narrowed.

"I'm here to help, sir!"

He sighed and pinched the bridge of his nose between thumb and forefinger. A weight filled my chest at the gesture. It felt like ants crawling around inside my skin. It was getting harder to breathe.

"Your mother wouldn't want you here."

I fought back the tears summoned by those words, knowing he was right.

"But you want me here, don't you sir?"

"That doesn't matter."

"Of course it matters!" I shouted at him. The cadets were staring at me now. The little girl having a tantrum on the battlefield.

"Go home, Paige." He seemed to loom over me, despite the fact we were the same height.

"But dad—"

"You haven't been trained, you don't know how to fly, you will only get in the way and get yourself hurt."

"Dad, I—"

"Get home NOW!"

I flinched away from his anger. He had never yelled at me like that. I hardly recognized the man before me.

He seemed to realize it, too. His eyes widened in shock as he stepped back. His arm reached toward me and he opened his mouth to speak, but I was already running.

I barreled right through a formation of new cadets, eliciting cries of outrage as I pushed past. I ran past the flights of upperclassmen, about to climb into their cockpits. I skirted around the seasoned officers, avoiding their disdainful looks. I shrugged past an outstretched hand attached to a flash of long cherry-red hair.

"Paige, wait!"

I didn't stop. Didn't even look toward the familiar girl's voice as I ran out of the hangar and into the connecting hallway that led to the military housing. My eyes blurred with tears, but I forced them down. I wouldn't let them fall. Not here. Not with everyone around. I didn't stop running until I got to the Officers' Quarters. I only paused there to swipe my ID card for entry before running up the stairs two at a time.

I flew through the front door of our housing unit. The metal panel crashed loudly against the frame, undoubtedly waking the neighbors. I didn't care. This whole building was too closely packed—the whole civilization. It made me feel claustrophobic.

"Honey, what's wrong?" My mother called from the worn brown leather couch. I didn't answer. Why would I? It wasn't really my mother, just a hologram. An artificial intelligence meant to sound like her. To look like her. To smell like her. To *replace* her.

It was meant to help with our grief. To help us heal from her untimely death. I hated the thing. What was the point of being human—of living—if we could be wrapped up into an AI program when we were gone? I didn't want to heal from the pain of losing her. I hoped to feel it forever. It was the last thing of hers that I had and I wasn't ready to give it up yet.

Once I let it go, she would truly be gone.

I ran past the door to my room and out the hallway window to the fire escape. Once outside, I started to climb. When I got to the roof, I collapsed on the old lawn chair where my mom used to sit while we looked at the stars. If I closed my eyes, I could almost imagine her there—holding me and stroking my hair as Dad named off each star. I could almost smell her perfume—though, that could have been the program, too.

In the solitude of my perfect roof hideaway, I started to cry.

Three

"What are you doing here, Paige?"

I said the words aloud, fully aware that talking to myself was a sign of insanity.

My first day at the academy hadn't gone exactly according to plan. Sure, I had trained for this since I was little, so physically I was more than ready. I had already outpaced most of my classmates in the entrance exam. It was the mental pressure I wasn't ready for. Everyone knew me as the Commander's kid. Half of the staff saw me as the little girl they knew from parties my parents hosted before my mom died. The other half hated me because they despised the Commander. On top of that, my classmates either thought I was here through nepotism and didn't deserve a chance at the pilot's seat, or that I was over-prepared, thanks to my father, and my presence wasn't fair to them. Little did they know the strained relationship I had with the Commander. I would much rather not be associated with him at all. Unfortunately, I couldn't just change my last name.

"Well, if it isn't little Paige Pearson."

The deep voice was none other than Tristan McDerman. Top ten of his class. Flight leader of Osprey flight. Second year at the academy. My superior and the boy I'd had a crush on since I was ten.

He was walking toward me with another pilot, both sporting blue flight suits. Tristan's green eyes and blond hair glowed in the bright sunlight, looking angelic compared to the dark brown hair of the boy beside him.

I bristled at his tone. "That's Cadet Pearson to you."

"Easy, Paige." Tristan laughed, ignoring my glare. "We're on the same side, remember."

"Wait, *Pearson*?" The dark-haired boy beside Tristan asked. His eyes widened. "You're the girl who stood up to Commander Pearson last year when he was still a Captain?"

"The very one," Tristan confirmed as I grimaced.

The dark-haired boy laughed, his hazel eyes sparkling with amusement. "You knocked me on my ass that day, Cadet."

"I . . . What?" Heat flushed my cheeks as I thought back to that day. "You were there?"

"It was my first day as a pilot." He laughed. "I was so embarrassed. My call sign was almost Timber because of you."

"Sorry," I muttered. "I don't know what I was thinking."

"You were being crazy," Tristan mocked.

13

"Shut up, Tristan," I snapped.

"I'd do what she says, Twist," the dark-haired boy said. I thought he was joking, but when I turned to him, deadly serious eyes stared at me from under dark lashes. "If she doesn't back down from Commander Pearson, you probably don't want to get on her bad side."

"Whatever." Tristan turned to me and smiled. It was cocky and disarming, just like him. I had to admit, after the day I had it was nice to see a familiar face. "She knows I'm only kidding. Don't you, Paige?"

I couldn't help but begrudgingly return his smile. I could never stay mad at him when he smiled at me like that—even when he was being a jerk. I nodded in acquiescence, but a strange weight formed in my stomach.

A buzz sounded over both the radios clipped to the boys' belts. A crackly voice filled the room.

"*Sky, you're needed in the command center.*"

To my surprise, the dark-haired boy raised his radio to his lips and pressed a button on the side. He was still watching me with interest. My eyes widened when he spoke, his voice spilling oddly from the speaker on Tristan's belt.

"On my way."

Callsign Sky? I swallowed hard. Shit, this was Skylar Monahue. Flight leader of Raptor flight—the best of the best. The youngest flight leader in history and first in his class. The pilot that saved hundreds of lives during the battle for Alba

Creek with his quick thinking and selflessness. *Everyone* had heard of Sky. He was a hero.

And I had knocked him over.

"Cadet Pearson." Skylar nodded to me as he left. I blinked at him, but he was gone before I could think of what to say.

When he disappeared behind a door, I rounded on Tristan. "Why didn't you tell me who that was?"

"Who, Sky?" Tristan smirked. "Why? Are you interested in him or something?"

"Of course not." I narrowed my eyes. "But I would have been a helluva lot more respectful had I known I was in the presence of cadet royalty!"

Tristan laughed and took my hand. "It's really good to see you, Paige."

I blushed as I looked down at our intertwined fingers. The intimate gesture filled my chest with warmth and drove all other thoughts from my mind. "It's good to see you, too."

Four

"What are you doing here, Paige?"

Tristan's annoyed voice sounded through the earpiece in my helmet. "Don't break formation. Get back to your wingmate!"

"Twister, you've got an enemy on your tail!" I called to him over the comms. "Use evasive maneuvers and I'll take care of them for you."

"Copy that," came Tristan's reply. He no longer sounded annoyed.

We may not have dated long—scratch that. Our attempt at dating may have been a bigger explosion than a downed aircraft in an oil field, but we still worked well together. We had to. He was still my flight leader and I didn't want him dead.

I shot the enemy plane with my laser and spared it barely a glance as it fell away from Tristan and crashed into the rocky ground far below.

"Thanks, Books," Tristan said. "Help me free up Hunter. She has two on her."

"Right behind you, Twist."

I fell into formation behind Tristan and we made our way through the air to where a member of our flight was being pursued by two enemy planes. The comms unit crackled to life in my ear as Tristan called out over the shared line.

"Hang in there, Hunter. Books and I are on your six."

"Finally!" she responded. Her voice was tight with poorly concealed anxiety. "I've been flying circles out here waiting for someone to assist!"

"Don't worry, Hunter," I said. "We've got your back!"

"Books, you take the one at 2 o'clock. I'll take the primary attacker," Tristan ordered. "Just like we practiced."

"Copy that."

I adjusted my heading to fall behind my assigned opponent. Seeing me on their instruments, they attempted evasive maneuvers. They veered away, abandoning their target and spiraling into a corkscrew to get away. They weren't as skilled as I was, however, and I dispatched them with my lasers halfway through a turn. I was about to level out and return to my wingmate when I heard Tristan's voice through my radio.

"Books, you've got a tail."

My stomach flipped and my heartbeat doubled in my chest. My palms grew clammy and my knuckles whitened as I tightened my grip on the controls. No matter how many times I heard the words, the reaction was the same. There was an enemy behind me with a target on my back. Would this be the last time I heard those words or could I out fly death again, today?

"I'm on my way to you," Tristan said. "Continue to evade and don't let them push you too high."

I pulled into a sharp turn and checked my readouts to see my altitude. I was already pretty high, but I wasn't *too* high. Pilots died when they flew too high. There's a point in the atmosphere where the air gets too thin. The plane malfunctions, the controls stop working, and the pilot is sent to a fiery death—either by enemy lasers or impact with the unforgiving ground.

I was a great pilot, even after only four years in the cockpit. I prided myself on my ability to outmaneuver almost any opponent, even those who had much more time behind the controls. To my surprise, however, my tail stayed on me. My jet shook around me as I took one sharp turn after another. Metal strained and groaned when I cut a sharp loop to the left, followed by a corkscrew to the right. I fought the g forces that pushed the blood down to my feet with every turn. I flew faster and faster, panic starting to affect my judgment. Angry red lasers shot past me, narrowly missing my wings and burning lines into my retinas. Surviving as a fighter pilot was a delicate mix of skill and luck, and if I couldn't shake this tail soon, my luck was going to run out.

This pilot was *good*. Not only could I not shake them, but they kept pushing me higher. I was nearing the top of my air column. Too much higher and I would leave the safe operating zone. I glanced up at the sky above me. The air was already so thin, I could almost see the stars beyond the atmosphere.

That gave me a crazy idea.

"I'm almost to you!" Tristan's voice seemed distant through my adrenaline fogged mind.

"There's only one way out of this, Twist," I said, setting my jaw and preparing.

"Do *not* attempt an upward loop, Books! I repeat, do NOT attempt! You are already too high."

I flipped to a private line. "Are you going to be here in the next ten seconds? If not, I'm dead, anyway."

There was silence on the line.

"What's your ETA, Tristan?!" I screamed as another laser narrowly missed my wing. Seconds. I only had seconds.

"Thirty seconds."

"That's not fast enough."

"Paige, no—"

I cut the line and pulled up hard. The g forces hit me like a physical weight as alarms lit up my cockpit. I squinted against the blackness encroaching on my vision and tried to force air into my lungs as every cell in my body screamed at me to stop this mad climb. My thoughts swam slowly through my mind, as if I was moving too fast for them to keep up. I kept my grip on the controls by sheer willpower and was rewarded with the sudden sight of my opponent before me.

With the tables turned, I shook off my adrenaline sickness. I wasn't out of danger. If I wanted to survive, I still had to focus. I shot my lasers at the jet and was almost surprised at the ease at which I hit them. I briefly mourned my opponent. No one had ever come that close to killing me before. The burning pieces of shrapnel falling to Earth could have easily been me, this time.

I was still forcing air into my lungs when I coasted into the hangar and popped my cockpit. Before I could climb out of my seat, I was met with the angry face of my flight leader. I looked past him to see a disgruntled Charles. Tristan must have pushed the engineer out of the way to climb up my flight ladder first.

"Are you okay?" Tristan looked me over as he helped me out of the cockpit. I swung myself onto the ladder and slid down the railing as I always did. I was a little shakier than usual as I hit the ground, but Charles steadied me before Tristan noticed. I shot him a grateful look as Tristan continued. "You look okay, which can't be right, because that was the dumbest thing you've ever done."

"Well, I'm alive," I retorted. "So that's something."

"I was almost to you—"

"You weren't close enough!" I snapped back.

"I was—"

"Cadet Pearson!"

The words snapped like a whip behind me, and even Tristan flinched from them. I closed my eyes for a second and took a deep breath before turning to face my father.

I forced myself into a salute as the Commander stormed up to me. His outrage was evident to anyone in a five mile radius. His black hair had lost the battle to the grays since I last saw him, but his eyes were still the same harsh blue.

"What the hell were you thinking?" he bellowed, loud enough for the entire hangar to overhear. I dropped my salute and took an involuntary step back. To his credit, Tristan stepped up beside me.

"Sir, if I—"

"Am I speaking to you right now, flight leader?" The Commander turned enraged eyes to Tristan.

"No, sir—"

"That's what I thought—"

"—but you are speaking to a member of my flight."

"No, flight leader," he said with an angry calm, turning back to me. "I am speaking to my daughter. You can step back, Osprey one."

Tristan nodded and took a step backward.

"See, Paige?" My dad gestured to Tristan. "This is how you follow orders. Why is that so hard for you?"

"Dad, I—"

"Why can't you follow simple directions?"

"I followed—"

"Why can't you do what your flight leader tells you and wait for him?"

"I would have—"

"Paige, explain to me why—"

"How can I tell you anything if you keep interrupting me?" I snapped.

My dad raised his eyebrows but waited for me to continue.

"I had already waited too long for backup. My tail was too good."

"You could have died, Paige. You went too high. Your equipment had already lost functionality. You weren't listening to your alarms. You weren't respecting your aircraft."

"I *would* have died had I not attempted that maneuver." I sighed and tried my best to explain. "I wasn't afraid, Dad. When I saw the stars—"

"The stars, Paige?" he asked, incredulously. "All this is about going to the stars? When will you grow up from this childish dream?"

"That's not what I was doing—"

"You need to focus on what's important. Your life and the lives of your flight members are more important. The lives of everyone in our civilization relies on you to focus on defending them."

"Dad, I—"

"If you can't even follow simple orders, you are never going to fly to the stars!"

The words hit me like a slap. Going to the stars wasn't a real goal—it was just a fantasy. I knew that. Our Civ didn't even have the technology to go to the stars, that knowledge was lost years ago. For some reason, though, his words struck me. Maybe, deep down, a part of me believed if I was good enough, I *would* go to the stars.

If I was the best soldier.

The best pilot.

The best daughter.

"Sir," Tristan found the nerve to step up again. "I don't appreciate the way you are speaking to a member of my flight."

I watched my father's resolve waver, then solidify. "I am no longer speaking to a member of your flight, Cadet."

What?

"Paige Pearson," The Commander said in a formal tone. "You are hereby relieved of your assignment to Osprey flight."

I shook my head and looked at Tristan. Blood drained from his face as he stared helplessly back at me. He was voiceless in the Commander's decision. In *my father's* decision. He couldn't prevent it, so he didn't move to interrupt the Commander.

"You are stripped of your position as pilot—"

"You're clipping my wings?" I asked in a daze. If I could never fly again—never feel the freedom of lifting off the tarmac and into the open air . . . but no. This was a bluff. He couldn't be serious.

23

"—You may continue to serve our community in other ways, but you may no longer do it from one of my cockpits."

"You're the *Commander*," I said, bewildered. "They're all your cockpits."

"Sir," Tristan tried again, "she's my best pilot. If you remove her from service, my flight will be—"

"Good pilots follow orders, do they not, flight leader?" my dad asked. The emotion was gone from his words. They were purely the words of the Commander now. Maybe this *wasn't* a bluff.

"I . . . Yes, sir," Tristan acquiesced.

"Pack up your belongings," my father said to me. "I'll expect you home for dinner."

With that, he turned and strode away.

I tore my eyes from the retreating figure and looked to Tristan, still unsure if this was really happening. Tristan blinked at me, then looked away, as if eye contact alone would get his wings clipped too. My lip curled in disgust and I turned away from him.

Despite the rage boiling beneath my skin at the injustice of it all, I walked calmly out of the hangar. I didn't look at my gawking flight mates, the sympathetic engineers, or to the jet that I would never fly again—it hurt too much. I pushed open the heavy metal man-door that led outside. I squinted while my eyes adjusted to the bright sunlight that reflected off the windows of the cadet's barracks before me. Only when the door clanged shut behind me, blocking me from view, did I start to run.

I hoped the physical activity would abate some of my anger, but the distance to my room was too short. I didn't bother slamming my door—all the other cadets were still out on the flight field being debriefed after today's skirmish. Instead, I threw my books from my tiny bookshelf, pages fluttering as bindings hit the floor. I stomped over them to get to the small armoire and started pulling out my flight suits, tossing them haphazardly around the room. I wouldn't need them anymore, anyway.

I stomped across the small room to my tidy desk, kicking anything unfortunate enough to be in my path. My desk was immaculately organized, with only a small figurine of a fighter jet resting on top. My father had gifted it to me upon passing my pilot's exam and it had sat in this place of honor since. I couldn't believe he thought I was just going to move back in with him after this. I didn't even want to look at him, let alone live beneath the same roof. There was no way I would live in the Officers' Quarters after having my wings clipped.

Screaming in frustration, I snatched up the little figurine and threw it against the wall. The ceramic jet shattered into a million pieces, a physical representation of my broken heart.

With nothing else to throw, I stared at the irreparable mess. My breathing turned from loud pants into quiet sobs as anger ebbed into despair. Without my wings, I was lost. I leaned back against the wall, then slid down to land hard on the floor. My eyes blurred with tears as I pulled my knees to my chest. I rested my forehead against my arms and cried.

Five

"Paige? What are you doing here?"

I started at the sound of the familiar voice. I looked up through watery eyes to see a woman with bright purple hair staring down at me. I scrubbed the tears from my cheeks before I could focus on her face, though the hair color gave away her identity, even before I recognized her features.

"Amara?"

"That's 'Captain Cassowary' to you, Cadet." She smiled to show me she was joking.

"You got a promotion?" I asked.

"I did."

"Congratulations, Captain." The words came out flat, despite the fact I actually was happy for her.

I saw her slip an envelope in her pocket as she stepped gingerly over the piles of my trashed belongings on the floor. She slid down the wall beside me and bumped her shoulder against mine. "Tell me about it, kiddo."

The term from my youth had fresh tears spilling down my cheeks. Amara was several years older than me. She had been in her last year of the academy when I started and had taken me under her wing.

"Haven't you heard?" I asked. "I'm not a pilot anymore."

"I heard you executed an extreme maneuver to escape certain death," Amara said. "I heard your father overreacted because you scared the shit out of him."

I perked up. "Can you talk to him? If you're a Captain . . ."

"You know once your father decides something, no one can change his mind."

I deflated. She was right. Even his generals couldn't talk him out of battle plans that he set into motion.

"Plus, I'm not exactly in his line of command."

"Wait, what?" I blinked at her, not comprehending. "He's the Commander of . . . everything."

"Not *quite* everything." Amara smiled.

She pulled the envelope from her pocket and handed it to me. I took it without thinking and stared down at the envelope. It had my name written on it in her elegant script. The back was sealed with wax and stamped with the word 'CONFIDENTIAL.' I looked up and she nodded for me to open it. I slid my finger through the seal to break it and pulled out the letter.

Cadet Paige Pearson,

You have been selected for admission to Dragon Flight by the Contact Initiative, a top-secret response to the extraterrestrial threat we are currently facing. Captain Amara Cassowary has recommended you become part of her team due to your response to danger while under pressure and your skill as a pilot—

The letter continued, but I looked up at Amara. "Is this for real?"

"I'm looking for a fighter who isn't afraid to push boundaries," Amara said. "I'm filling my team with the best of the best. I want you on that team."

I stared at her, then at the letter. "Extraterrestrials? Aliens?"

"You told me once you wanted to go to the stars. Is that still true?"

To the stars. The battle cry from when I was younger still resonated with me. Yes, I did still want to go to the stars. Even more so now, since doing so would piss off the Commander.

"You don't have to give me your answer now," Amara said. "I was going to leave this letter under your door. Take the day to decide." She stood and looked down at me. "Being a pilot isn't something you can just stop, Paige. Once a pilot, always a pilot."

She walked to the door, but paused when I called out to her.

"Captain Cassowary!" I said, jumping to my feet. "Count me in."

She turned to me and smiled. "Well then, you better pack your bags."

After grabbing the few things I wanted to keep from my destroyed room, I followed Amara out of the Cadet's barracks. We walked to a small, nondescript door that looked to be attached to a maintenance shed. When Amara swiped her keycard, the door opened to a small room with a rusty metal staircase leading down. The door slammed shut behind us and fluorescent light bulbs hummed to life, illuminating the simple room with yellow light.

"We're going underground?" I asked, eying the staircase skeptically as she started the descent.

"I don't know if you've noticed, but there isn't a lot of space up here. This was the only place we could think of to keep this program secret."

"Why is it secret?" I followed her down, wincing at each creak the staircase emitted, ready to grab the railing if my foot fell through a particularly rusty spot.

"We didn't want to cause panic with the thought of alien invasion." We reached the bottom of the steps and she swiped her card again. The light on the card reader turned green and she twisted the handle. "And we didn't want to get people's hopes up if our plans fell apart."

She opened the door to another world. We walked out onto a balcony overlooking a massive hangar. Instead of the dull gray I was accustomed to from decades of exhaust clinging to the walls, this hangar was shiny and new. Engineers in green jumpsuits intermingled with pilots in blue flight suits as was typical, but instead of fighter jets, a different type of craft lined this hangar. The sleek aircraft looked like a mix between a jet and a spaceship. The wings curved back into sharp points and the weaponry mounted to the turrets were like nothing I'd ever seen before.

"Whoa."

"Yep." Amara nodded. "Just wait 'til you sit in one. These cruisers fly like a dream. They don't rattle around like the jets you're used to."

"What's mounted on the nose?"

"A different sort of laser. New design that works in the absence of atmosphere."

"Wait, these things can leave the atmosphere?"

"In theory," she said. "We've only tested them to the mesosphere, but once we have a team assembled, we want to go further."

The cruiser had a deadly graceful silhouette, but it was the idea of space travel that had me itching to climb inside one. I was about to say so when I heard yet another familiar voice from down below.

"Finally, Songbird! I've been waiting for you to recruit my wingmate!"

I turned to the voice and was shocked to see Skylar Monahue smiling up at us. His dark brown hair was longer than the last time I had seen him—it fell past his ears now—but his hazel eyes were the same.

"I should have given you some warning," Amara called down to him, causing me to jump. I had forgotten her callsign was Songbird, though it made sense with her brightly colored hair that changed every month. She gestured for me to follow her down a flight of stairs to where Skylar was waiting below. "Looks like you could use a shave. Sky, how long have you been working?"

Skylar rubbed the scruff on his face and grimaced as if he had just noticed it. Now that we were closer, I could see several days of growth on his chin. He was much shorter than I remembered, too. He was still a few inches taller than me, but the first time I had met him as a cadet, I thought he was so tall. So much better than me. Untouchable.

Wait . . . did he say I was *his* wingmate?

"You know, I'm not sure." He thought for a moment. "What day is it? I get so mixed up down here."

"It's Thursday morning," Amara said.

"Ah . . . Yeah. I've been here too long." He shrugged. "You know how it is, Songbird. This stuff is so cool, sometimes I just get carried away."

"I know. I'm hoping Books here can keep you under control," Amara said, wryly.

"Have you met Cadet Pearson?" Skylar smiled and shifted his gaze to me. "She works just as hard as I do."

Surprised he remembered my name, I could only raise my eyebrows at the compliment.

"Yes," Amara said, "but she's smarter than you. I've never seen her forget to eat for so long she needed to be admitted to medical for dehydration."

Another compliment? If I spent too long down here, I was going to grow an ego.

"I get really focused, sometimes," Skylar said to me, as if that was a valid reason for not eating. "It's good to see you again, Books. You wanna see the cruisers?"

I still hadn't found my voice, so I nodded.

"Great! Follow me." He smiled and my stomach did a weird little flip at the expression. It seemed I was still a little starstruck.

He led me over to one of the cruisers in the lineup. Amara started to follow but was distracted by an engineer with a clipboard asking her a question. I felt a little bad leaving her behind, but I *really* wanted to get a closer look at that aircraft.

"This is Dragon Six."

We walked up to the sixth cruiser in the lineup and I gawked openly.

"She's beautiful." I stepped up beside the sleek black hull and reached my hand out. I paused before I made contact and turned back to Skylar. "May I?"

"By all means." He nodded.

I grinned and turned back to the matte-black cruiser, reaching up to run my hand along the underside of the nose.

The exterior was a smooth, rubbery material. I inspected the laser mechanism and was astounded that I couldn't follow the design. I knew everything about my jet—from the engine maintenance to the weaponry—but this cruiser was on another level entirely.

"What's it made of?"

"Some sort of highly confidential stealth material," Skylar said. "It can't be picked up by basic radar and the color is sexy as hell."

It really was. "Are you the flight leader?"

"No, that would be Songbird."

I tore my gaze from the cruiser to look back at him. "Really? Amara?"

"You're surprised?" Sky raised his eyebrows. "She's a great pilot."

"Yeah, but so are you."

"Thank you." He smiled at me and I turned back to the cruiser before he noticed my blush. "I am a good pilot, but I'm not as good at organization. A flight leader needs to be able to multitask. I am definitely lacking in that area compared to her."

I remembered what he had said about forgetting to eat, and I was inclined to agree with him.

"Plus," he continued, "she's better at talking to the other Civ leaders."

I turned back to him, all embarrassment forgotten. "She talks to the other Civs? How? Why?"

"Look around, Pearson." Skylar gestured to the hangar around us. "Do you think we came up with all this on our own? The Contact Initiative has been a joint effort between all the Civs since before the fighting started."

"If we're working with the other Civs . . . why are we still fighting them?"

Skylar shrugged. "We're separate from the general military. We have no control over them. They keep fighting amongst themselves while we work in secret to protect the entire human race."

"Does the military know about this program?"

"Yes," Skylar said. His sad expression said he knew what I was really asking.

Does my dad know about this program?

My dad knew how close we were to space travel. He knew we had the technology to travel the stars. He knew—and he still clipped my wings.

"And they're okay with us working with other Civs?" I asked, changing the direction of the conversation. "Even while they kill each other?"

"I don't know if they're *okay* with it, but they know it won't matter who wins our civil war if the aliens just come and wipe out the winners."

Our conversation lapsed as I contemplated what he said. My mind flashed back to this morning, the image of burning scrap falling to the ground. The destroyed jet could have easily been my own. A human life was in that jet—a life that I ended. Every enemy I shot down over the years . . . Was all that death truly pointless?

Skylar somehow seemed to sense the shift in my mood. I'm not sure how he knew, but he said the only thing that could have pulled me out of my thoughts.

"Do you want to sit in it?"

I turned around to see Skylar at the bottom of the steps leading to the cockpit. He was leaning against the railing with his hands shoved into the pockets of his flight suit. He laughed as I grinned and darted past him in answer.

He followed me up the stairs and showed me how to pop open the glass dome over the cruiser's cockpit. I slid into the contoured pilot's seat and my eyes widened as I looked around at the controls. They were vaguely similar to the ones in my jet, but much more complicated.

Skylar seemed to read my mind as he leaned into the cockpit from the top of the stairs.

"As you can see, all the components from the jets are here. They fly basically the same, but there's a lot more power in these babies." He patted the side of the cruiser lovingly as he spoke. "You'll have to take it easy on your turns until you get the hang of it. You don't want to pass out doing simple maneuvers. Trust me, you will never hear the end of it."

"It's so advanced," I said, awe hushing the sound of my voice. "If all the Civs have this technology, why don't we use it to fight each other?"

"Two reasons. The first being this tech is crazy expensive." Skylar grimaced. "They wouldn't want us destroying this stuff just to fight other humans. The second reason is we aren't allowed. There's some sort of agreement in place between the Civs. We can only use this against alien invasion."

"Alien invasion. Is that likely? Have we actually made contact with aliens?"

"Contact, yes. Invasion . . ." Skylar shrugged. "We don't know much about the extraterrestrials other than they have *much* more advanced technology than we do."

"So the invasion isn't likely, just a possibility."

"Well, I didn't say that. I'm pretty sure we insulted them in the last transmission."

I blinked. "Why would we do that?"

"We're human," Skylar said wryly. "We like to fight things."

I looked at the switches and dials before me. Instead of seeing the shiny hangar walls, I imagined myself flying among the stars, fighting aliens alongside people from other Civs. I shook my head. The thought was unreal. Outlandish.

"You really fly this thing?" I asked.

He smirked. "No, I fly that one." He pointed to the cruiser next to mine labeled Dragon Five. "Dragon Six is yours."

I blinked at him, then looked back at the controls. The swelling of emotion made it hard to breathe as I gently trailed my finger over the instruments. Dragon Six was *mine*. Tears threatened to spill from my eyes again. Had it been only earlier today that my own father had clipped my wings? I thought I would never fly again. Now I was sitting in the most advanced cockpit I'd ever seen in a cruiser that was designed for *space travel*. I looked up at my new wingmate—the best pilot of our generation—and had to wipe away a tear.

"I–I'm sorry, I . . ." I didn't know what to say.

"Hey, it's okay." Sky rested a hand gently on my shoulder. It was oddly comforting considering I hardly knew him. "I get it. I heard what the Commander did, and I'm sorry. I'm sure it's been an emotional day, and this is a lot to take in."

"Yeah, it is a lot."

"Are you having second thoughts about joining?" he asked.

"Absolutely not! It's always been my dream to travel the stars. I wouldn't miss this opportunity for anything."

He smiled and his eyes sparkled as he gave my shoulder a soft squeeze. "Welcome to the team, wingmate."

A warmth filled my chest as his welcome started to weld the shattered pieces of my heart.

Six

"What are you doing here, Paige?"

Skylar blinked and unsuccessfully tried to stifle a yawn. I leaned against the doorframe of his room and bit my lip. He was in nothing but boxers and his hair was sticking up on one side.

"Oh, you were sleeping." I forced myself to look at his face and not the exposed skin of his chest and stomach. "I-I'm sorry. I'll go."

"Wait, Books." Skylar reached out and took my elbow before I could flee. "I'm up now. What's up?"

"You said I could talk to you about anything." I looked down at my hands. "Did you mean that?"

"Of course."

I looked down the hallway, wondering if anyone else was up at this hour. Sky followed my gaze and seemed to realize we were just standing in the hallway.

"Oh, sorry." He backed up and gestured for me to follow him. "Come on in."

I walked into his room and just sort of stood in the center, looking around. He shut the door behind me and I suddenly felt awkward. The small room looked just like mine, but it was cluttered with half-finished drawings of cruiser designs and flight patterns. Sky was so clever. He was always coming up with ideas for the flight team. He could have been an amazing engineer had he not wanted to be a pilot. He told me he often stayed up all night trying to get the ideas out of his head. He got so little sleep these days.

And I had just woken him.

"I'm really sorry, Sky. I didn't mean to . . ."

"No worries." He grabbed a shirt from a half open drawer and slid it on. I could suddenly breathe a little easier. "I'm sure I wouldn't have been sleeping much longer anyway. I was having the weirdest dream about—" His eyes met mine and color tinted his cheeks. "Uh, never mind."

He tried to put his hands in his pockets, but his boxers didn't have any. Instead, he rested them on his hips. Then, looking uncomfortable he wrung his hands together. He was just as awkward as me. It was cute.

I blushed at the direction of my thoughts and looked away.

"Sorry," Sky said. "Please, sit wherever."

I nodded and walked over to sit on the bed. Only when I perched myself on the edge of his mattress did I find the courage to look at him. He studied me for a long moment before walking over and sitting beside me. He swallowed once, then cleared his throat.

"So, uh . . . what's wrong?"

"Nothing," I said automatically.

"Paige." He raised an eyebrow at me. "It's three in the morning and you're in my room."

"Maybe I'm just into you." I said it like a joke, but my face heated.

"Maybe." Sky smirked. "But I feel like there's more to it than that. Something must be wrong."

I sighed and picked at a loose thread on my sweatpants. "You know, I'm just so used to pretending to be fine all the time, I just . . . I don't know how to—"

I cut off when the warmth of his hand encircled mine.

"You don't have to pretend for me." His hazel eyes held mine and I felt my cheeks warming. When he noticed my blush, he dropped my hand. "Sorry, I . . . I mean it, though. You can talk to me about anything. I won't judge you or scold you or . . . whatever your dad did."

I looked back at the loose thread.

"It must have been tough growing up with a military dad," he said.

"You have no idea."

"Tell me about it?"

I looked at him. He sounded serious, so I nodded.

"He did his best, but he was impossible to please. I always tried, but nothing was ever good enough." I shook my head. "I was always getting into trouble trying to impress him."

"I bet he was strict."

I shrugged. "Yeah, he was pretty strict when he was around, but most of the time, my mom raised me."

"What was she like?"

I smiled as I pictured her face. "She was the sweetest person in the world. She was quiet, but strong. She had her own beliefs. She and my dad would argue for hours over politics and the best path for our Civ to take forward. She was the only person I've ever known that could change my dad's mind, but let me tell you, it was a huge effort on her part. I don't know why she stayed with him, to be honest." I sighed. "I miss her."

"She seems great."

"We got one of those AI replicators, you know. After she died, I mean."

Skylar's brows shot up. "How was that?"

"Terrible." I shivered. "Whoever came up with that idea should be executed. Or put on permanent bathroom cleaning duty, or something."

"Yeah, that's one piece of technology that never should have been created. I feel like it traumatizes more than it helps." He shook his head. "I'm sorry you had to go through that."

"Thanks." I huffed a sardonic laugh. I came here to talk, but I couldn't talk about my mom, anymore—not without risking tears. "What about your parents?"

"What about them?"

"I've never heard you talk about them. Are they still . . ."

"Alive?" He nodded. "Yeah. They live up north in Research Station Beta. I haven't seen them in . . . a while."

"Will you tell me about them?"

"Sure." He smiled and his eyes took on a faraway look. "My parents are scientists—they met at the agricultural lab. My brother and I grew up running around the labs. We were surrounded by intellectuals who pushed us to be inquisitive—to always ask questions and find our own answers." He grimaced. "I think my parents are disappointed I joined the military."

"What? How could they be disappointed? You're the best pilot we have."

He shrugged, then scooted back to lean against his headboard. "They're pacifists. They don't think anyone in the military has the freedom to make decisions—to make advances. If only they could see what I'm doing now." He looked at the papers scattered around his room. "They wanted me to go into bioengineering, you know."

I moved next to him and rested my shoulder against his. For some reason, I just really needed the contact. I was grateful he didn't pull away.

"So why didn't you?"

"My brother was killed in that bombing a few years back. I had just turned sixteen, so I enlisted. My parents were pissed, but I just thought . . . what if I could have protected him? Research just seemed so useless in light of his death."

I leaned my head on his shoulder. "I'm sorry about your brother."

"Thanks." After a moment, he put his arm around me. "At least I didn't have to deal with that AI bullshit."

I snorted a laugh.

"Count yourself lucky." I relaxed into him, resting my head against his chest. His heartbeat was a soothing rhythm in my ear as I closed my eyes and breathed him in. "Sky?"

"Yeah?"

"What were you dreaming about? Before I so rudely woke you up."

There was a long pause. I heard his heart skip a beat before he answered.

"You." He rested his head on top of mine and I felt him sigh into my hair. "This."

"Ah, so it was a good dream." I smiled as warmth filled my chest.

"Oh, Pearson," Skylar chuckled and tightened his arm around me. "You're always knocking me on my ass."

Seven

"What are you doing here, Paige?"

Skylar's voice in my headset shook me out of my daze. I had been staring at the flight hundreds of meters below as they fell under more and more enemy fire. Eagle Flight—My father's flight.

The aliens had been persistent enough in their attacks recently that the general military had called for a ceasefire amongst civilizations. As ill prepared and cobbled together as they were, the fighter jets had started helping us defend the Earth from the invaders. I looked out the right side of my cruiser to see Skylar coasting alongside me. I couldn't see his face under his helmet, but I could imagine the concerned expression he was wearing.

"Get down there and help them," he continued on our private line. "I'll cover for you up here."

I could have kissed him.

"Thank you, Sky!" I tipped my nose down into a steep dive and sped toward my father.

"Books, where are you going?" Amara called through our flight line. I didn't answer, but Sky's voice sounded, covering for me like he promised.

"Just a pre-approved rescue mission, Songbird."

"Pre-approved? By whom?"

"Me and Books, obviously," he scoffed through the line.

"I don't recall either of you being qualified to make those decisions."

"Hey, you knew what you were getting when you recruited us."

I tuned out their banter as I approached Eagle Flight. I knew which one was my father based on his flight leader placement in the formation. He also happened to be the one shooting tails off everyone else with no concern for the growing amount of enemies chasing him. The alien's strange lasers kept missing the important parts of his jet, but they were close enough to leave marks on his hull. I was impressed he had been able to survive this long with so many enemies shooting at him.

"Eagle One," I called through the wider communication system so he could hear me, "you have seven enemies on your tail. I recommend evasive maneuvers."

"Paige?" my father asked, as if I could have been anyone else. He sounded like he couldn't believe his ears. True, I hadn't spoken to him since he clipped my wings, but it wasn't like the tenor of my voice had changed. He knew it was me.

I rapidly shot my laser at his line of tails and succeeded in striking two of them. I had to swerve to avoid the shrapnel of the exploding ships. The alien crafts had many advantages over us, but flying in atmosphere was not one of them. "Correction—five enemies."

I fired again and hit one more before the rest scattered to find easier prey.

"I think you're clear, Eagle One." I got an alert on one of my displays, indicating he was trying to open a private line to my comms. I pressed a few buttons, accepting the transmission.

"Thank you, Paige. I—" His voice crackled like broken glass over the speaker, and I couldn't tell if it was him or the comms. It sounded like he wanted to say more, but there was a long pause on the line. "That was some impressive shooting."

I knew I would never get the apology I wanted, even though I could practically hear it in his voice. That was okay. I didn't need him—not anymore. I knew I was where I was supposed to be. I was a Dragon. I flew with the best pilots in history. I didn't get my self-worth from anyone but myself. Not anymore.

The realization made me feel lighter.

"Thanks, Dad," I said. "I learned from the best."

"I've got it handled down here, Paige. Be careful."

"You too, Dad."

I tipped my nose to the sky and headed back to my flight in the upper atmosphere. By the time I arrived, Dragon Flight was already gone—all except for one.

"Ready, Books?" Skylar's voice was like a welcome home in the private line of my helmet.

"Ready, Sky." I smiled, although I knew he couldn't see it.

"Then let's get going! We're already miles behind the others!"

"Alright, alright! Let's go!" I couldn't contain my own excitement as I tipped my cruiser's nose toward the sky. I glanced out from my cockpit to the sleek shape of Sky's cruiser beside my own. "Hey, Sky?"

"Yeah?"

"Thanks for waiting."

"Always, Pearson."

I flipped off my mic and took a breath, settling myself. I looked at the deep expanse of shimmering pinpricks of light before me—and smiled. I felt lighter than I had in a long time. Since before my father clipped my wings. Since before joining Tristan's flight. Since before my mother's death. Probably all the way back to those nights on the roof during blackouts, when my father would point out each star and name them. On the brink of achieving my childhood goal, I allowed myself to feel joy.

I allowed myself to be happy.

"To the stars."

Sky's the Limit

Through the Rift Publishing

One

"Skylar, wait up!"

I paused in the hallway to wait for my younger brother. "Hurry up, Silas. We're going to miss Dr. Roe's lecture on plant vascular systems."

"That sounds so boring." Silas huffed. "Don't you know enough about plants, already?"

"We recovered viable plant life from a meteorite that clearly shows us how plants interact with chemicals around them. Dr. Roe's recent breakthrough on gas exchange could revolutionize the way we—"

Silas' eyes glazed over so I knew he was no longer listening. He was only a year younger than me, but at fifteen, I was already working in Dr. Roe's lab full time. The survival of the human race in the desolate landscape we inhabited had pushed me to specialize, whereas Silas just didn't care about the future. He was still bouncing around the different departments, not interested in committing to anything. That was probably my fault—as his older brother, it was my responsibility to be a role model, after all. Silas was my best friend, but even I didn't know what he really wanted.

I sighed. "I could just talk to Dr. Roe about it later . . ."

"Really?" Silas' face lit up. "Can we go ride the bikes on the roof?"

"We got in trouble for that last time." I looked around the hallway, empty save for the potted plants lining the walls. "But if everyone is in the lecture . . ."

"Yes!" He grabbed my hand and pulled me toward the stairs.

"Where was this energy before?"

"Not wasted on plants," Silas scoffed.

I rolled my eyes but let him tow me into the stairwell.

The rooftop had been converted into a greenhouse with rows upon rows of plants. It spanned the entire length of the massive Research Station and held both food growth operations and select experiments. Some of Dr. Roe's projects were up here, so I spent a lot of my working hours in the quarantine room. Miles of trails had been cultivated as walking paths up here—nothing like the end of the world to spur health reform.

The scientists that worked up here had electric bikes, but they were locked down for official use only. "No joyrides, whatsoever," according to Sheriff Larz. That didn't stop us from overriding the access codes.

We cruised the trails—the joy of relative freedom filled me to the brim and erupted in laughter. The wind roared in my ears as plants whipped past. I relished the crunch of gravel beneath my tires, the spray of the sprinklers in my face, and even the sting of thorns against my arms. I craved action and activity, though my childhood had been one of books and lectures. I dreamed of the adventures I read about, even while being told to never leave the Station.

Too soon, we had to stop. The battery indicators on our bikes flashed red, so we found an electrical box on an outer wall to charge them. We had to crawl under a few tables to plug them in, but it was worth it. It would've been a long walk home, otherwise.

"What's that?" Silas pointed to a green cloth hanging on the wall.

We jogged over to inspect it. It was camouflaged well enough that we wouldn't have seen it from the trail, especially speeding by on our bikes. Silas pulled back the sheet to look behind it and revealed a rusty metal sheet on the wall with a glass cut out at eye level.

"Is that a door?" I gasped. "To the outside?"

He grinned at me. "One way to find out!"

"Silas, wait—"

It was too late. Silas had already pushed open the door, letting in a gust of warm, dry air. Nothing bad happened. No alarms went off. I let out a breath—we were okay.

We crept out onto a small balcony and I shaded my eyes against the bright sunlight. Food wrappers and drink containers littered the space. Someone was obviously using this balcony for something. Hopefully, that meant it wouldn't crumble away beneath our feet.

Desert stretched as far as I could see. Railroad tracks extended from the Station into the distance and sparse clusters of plants dotted the landscape, but it was mostly just . . . nothing. I could count on my fingers the number of times I had been outside in my life. The absence of walls to ground me was dizzying.

"Look!" Silas gripped the railing and pointed at the sky. Five dots moved slowly across the sky in a V formation.

"Are those jets?"

"Must be picking up an emergency shipment."

I nodded. That was rare, but it happened. Usually after a bad battle or if the railroads had been compromised. I hadn't heard anything, though. Not that they would have told a couple of kids.

We stared up into the sky that we rarely got to see. The outdoors were not safe. We had it drilled into us from the time we could crawl, even though the risk of attack here was less than other places. Perks of the Research Stations serving multiple Civs—they all knew where their food came from. If we went down, the Civilizations would suffer.

"You ever thought about leaving, Kye? Going to one of the other Civs. Seeing what's out there."

I blinked. "Have you?"

"All the time."

I turned to him. He was frowning at the sky.

"What would you do, Si?"

"I dunno. Flying one of those fighter jets would be cool."

"The military? Really?"

"Just think of it, Kye." Silas closed his eyes and lifted his face toward the sun. "The wind in your hair. The sun on your skin. The whole world flashing by below you. The freedom to go wherever you want."

The way he described it sounded liberating. Like the feeling of riding a bike, but infinitely better. And to go outside whenever you wanted? Not to be trapped in a lab all day like one of the lab rats? It sounded like a dream come true.

But that wasn't how the military worked. There was constant fighting and death. According to our parents, the military was the reason we had to live like we did—cut off from nature and hiding in our self-made prisons.

I shook my head. "Mom and Dad would disown you."

Silas gave a derisive laugh.

"Seriously, Si, you'd kill someone? Because that's what you'd have to do in the military. Mom and Dad—"

"Mom and Dad aren't right all the time." Silas looked at me sideways. "The military was formed to protect us. Sure, maybe they have to do some bad things, but . . . what about Larz? He's technically part of the military. Do you see him killing everything in his path?"

"Well, no . . ."

The Sheriff was a pain most of the time, but I'd never seen him hurt anyone. His job was to keep order and protect. I respected him for it, even when he ratted on us to our parents for breaking a few tiny rules.

"I just feel like there's gotta be more out there." Silas leaned against the rickety railing and sighed. "I have to fit in somewhere, don't I?"

"You fit in here, Silas." That earned me another sideways look. I shrugged. "Okay, well, you fit in with me."

He laughed.

I had always been good at spotting patterns and their variations. It's why I was good at analyzing data—I could see the patterns in the numbers. Maybe that's why I noticed right away when a sixth dot broke off from the V formation of jets and started coming our way.

"Si, is that another jet?"

Silas looked up and the color drained from his face.

"No, I don't think it is."

We exchanged wide-eyed looks and bolted for our bikes. I ripped the power cords from the electrical supply and pulled the red lever beside it. An alarm screamed over my head. They would be blaring through the entire Station, alerting everyone of the danger. Silas had started up both of our bikes and was waiting for me on the trail. Our panicked ride to the stairwell was nothing like the fun-filled experience we had earlier. Halfway there, my bike slowed. It didn't have enough time to charge while we were outside, so I jumped off and ran. Silas stayed beside me on his bike, even though I yelled at him to keep going. His bike didn't last much longer.

We ran together. My heart was in my throat and my lungs burned. I cursed myself for letting the bikes' batteries get so low in the first place. I should have made us stop to charge them earlier. I was an adult, damnit. I should have been more responsible. I shouldn't have agreed to skip the lecture to come up here and—

I felt the shock wave before I heard the explosion. It pushed me to the ground. Dirt and broken pots rained down over me. I curled up in a ball and covered my head with my arms. I could do nothing but hope and breathe as my entire world crumbled around me.

Eventually, the dirt-rain stopped falling. I opened my eyes to the ruined greenhouse. A gaping hole tore through the ceiling behind me. The floor opened up to several levels below. Water gushed from broken pipes and smoke rose from one of the labs below. I scrambled away from the edge.

"Silas?" My voice was scratchy and speaking made me cough. "Silas! Where are you?"

There was no answer.

"Silas!" I screamed into the hole.

"Here!"

His weak reply came from behind me.

I spun around. "Silas, where—"

My voice died in my throat. He was only feet from the ledge, pinned under a fallen beam. Blood leaked from the corner of his mouth as he grimaced up at me.

"I could use a hand, Kye."

I ran to him and heaved against the huge piece of metal holding him down. It didn't budge. I looked around for something I could use. A metal shovel lay in the rubble nearby. I grabbed it, then wedged it beneath the beam to use as a lever against a broken block of concrete. The beam shifted. Silas screamed. I dropped the shovel and ran to him. Blood began to pool beneath him.

"I'm sorry." My hands shook as I cradled his head. "I-I don't know what to do."

"Go get help." Silas' eyes were clear, despite the pain he had to be in. "You can't lift the whole building by yourself, no matter how much you want it."

"Alright. I'll go get help." I wiped the blood from his chin with my sleeve. "Hang on, Si. You're gonna be okay."

Silas closed his eyes and I ran faster than I thought possible. I took the steps three at a time and collided with Sheriff Larz on his way up the stairwell. I bounced off of him, but he steadied before I hit the ground.

"Sheriff!" I grabbed his hand and pulled him up the steps. "My brother! He's trapped!"

The Sheriff bolted up the steps, beating me to the roof.

"There!" I pointed toward Silas. His limp body looked so tiny half-buried below the rubble.

We only got a few steps into the greenhouse when the building shook. Was that another bomb? No, the building was unstable. The partially collapsed roof was deteriorating. Pieces of the floor crumbled away and crashed into the hole.

The floor under Silas fell.

Silas screamed.

I lunged for him, but Larz caught me around the waist.

"No!" I screamed as I struggled. The Sheriff's grip never wavered as he pulled me pack to the stairwell. "Silas!"

Sheriff Larz loomed over me in the medical bay. I sat quietly in a folding chair, watching the haggard staff rush between hastily erected cots. Warm tears still leaked from my eyes and . . . my ears? I touched my earlobe and pulled my hand away. Dried blood crusted my fingertips. Weird that I didn't feel any pain.

"Skylar!" Mom's shrill voice cut through the voices buzzing around me. She pulled me into a crushing embrace. "Thank goodness. Where's your brother?"

I didn't know what to say.

"Larz, where's Silas?" Dad's voice sounded distant to my damaged ears.

"I found the boys up in the greenhouse." Larz closed his eyes and shook his head. "I'm sorry, by the time I got there—"

Dad grabbed my shoulders and shook me.

"What were you doing up there?" he screamed. My voice completely fled. "You should have been with us."

"Issac, stop!" Mom pulled Dad off of me.

Dad looked at his hands, horrified, then bolted. Mom looked at me, tears streaming down her face. After a quick word with Larz, she followed dad out of the med-bay. Larz let out a deep breath and sat beside me.

"Did you pull that alarm, Skylar?"

I looked up at the Sheriff. Somehow I managed a nod.

"That was quick thinking, kid. You saved a lot of lives today."

Not the one that mattered.

"Sheriff?" My throat burned. It was the first word I'd spoken since screaming my brother's name.

"Yeah?" Larz studied me with wary eyes. He was probably worried I would pass out. Or maybe explode. There'd been enough explosions for one day.

"How do I become a pilot?"

Larz leaned back in his chair. "You want to be a pilot?"

"Yes."

"Like the one that took your brother?"

"Yes."

There was a strained silence between us. Larz looked me up and down. I was covered in dirt and scratches, but my head was oddly clear. Not even the usual distractions bothered me.

"You sure, kid?"

I refused to be that helpless ever again. "I'm sure."

Larz nodded. "I'll make a call."

Two

The alarm blared in the hallway and for a moment I was sixteen again, running for my life from a bomb, Silas beside me. Aggravated voices and the scramble of footsteps past my door brought me back to the present. My brother's death was seven years ago. A lifetime.

I looked at my clock and groaned. It had only been three hours since Dragon Flight had returned from our scouting mission. Two hours since I crawled into bed. Thirty minutes since I finally fell asleep.

Murphy's damn Law.

I heaved myself out of bed, pulling on a clean flight suit. There were no drills anymore—this wasn't flight school. The aliens attacking our planet didn't care about my insomnia.

I opened my door to find Paige waiting for me just outside. My wingmate leaned against the doorframe, lips set into a grim line.

Strong, brave, fierce.

Dark circles shadowed her electric blue eyes and she stifled a yawn. I stepped into the hallway and pulled my door shut behind me.

"Morning, Sky," she said while I locked my door.

"Is it?"

I took a few steps in the direction of the cruiser bay, but my palms started to itch. I locked my door, right? I wouldn't be able to stop thinking about it if I didn't check. Paige didn't move until I rushed back to confirm. Then she pushed away from the wall and matched my stride down the hallway.

"I think so." She ran a hand through her short black hair. It was a little tangled, but a few brushes of her hand tamed it back to normal. "I haven't actually looked at the time. It's a little trick I learned in flight school. If I don't know how much sleep I got, I can convince my body to function properly."

I smiled despite my fatigue. "I'll have to try that next time."

We got to the end of the hall in time to see our Flight Leader scramble out of her room. She struggled to tie her mess of orange and green tinted hair back into a presentable bun.

"Amara," Paige called to her. "Do you know what's happening?"

Amara—callsign Songbird, due to her ever-changing hair color—paused for us to catch up. She shrugged and fell into step beside us.

"I doubt they'll send us out. We only got back three hours ago."

"Three hours?" Paige groaned and rubbed her face. "I was at dinner with the girls for at least an hour."

I put my hand on Paige's shoulder; partly for moral support, partly to steer her around a corner, since she wasn't looking where she was going.

"The other flights are doing well in training. My guess is Commander Shale will send one of them to deal with whatever this is."

I was skeptical. The newly forged Phoenix and Griffin Flights were still getting to know their cruisers. It took Dragon Flight months to figure out how to fly as a unit in the newer and more powerful spaceship designs. Not to mention how to even start to fight outside the Earth's atmosphere. Battles in zero gravity were totally different from what normal pilots were used to.

When we got to the door of the main cruiser bay, Paige pulled me to a stop. She reached up to flatten my hair—I hadn't even spared it a thought.

"Thanks." I hoped she didn't notice what her proximity did to me.

"Hurry up, you two!" Amara called from where the others were already waiting.

We rushed over and formed up, standing at attention. I was the only guy in our flight, which was some sort of an anomaly. Dragon Flight was the best of the best—hand-picked to trailblaze the Contact Initiative. Gender didn't play into it.

We didn't wait long for orders. Commander Shale emerged from a doorway with a frown and a clipboard. He glanced over the assembled crews. Stragglers were filling in from all directions, but he didn't wait for them to find their places.

"Attention!" The commander's voice boomed over the low murmur of the crowd. Someone had silenced the alarms. "We've received word of an ongoing attack on one of the Research Stations to the north. This Agricultural station is crucial to the survival of the human race."

My hands went cold and I wasn't the only one holding my breath. The crowd around me was absolutely silent.

"Eighty percent of our food and most of our agricultural advancement comes from this Station," the commander continued. "It is unclear how the enemy knows this, but they are focusing their attacks there. We will be joining this battle, we will protect Research Station Beta, and—"

The world slowed down around me and a high pitch rang in my ears. Light-headed, I drifted, unmoored from my own skin. Beta was *my* Station. It was where my brother died. Where my parents still lived—maybe not for long.

The world snapped back into motion at a pressure in my hand. I looked down to see Paige clutching it, her eyes shining with concern.

Think, Skylar. Think.

I was already walking to my cruiser.

"Hold up, Sky," Amara called. "We haven't been assigned to—"

"We're going." I didn't recognize the flat, emotionless voice as my own.

"Request the assignment, Songbird." Paige was beside me in a second, heading to her cruiser. "You heard Sky. We're going."

I heard Amara's groan, but didn't wait to see if she argued. I took the steps to Dragon Five two at a time and climbed into the cockpit. As the glass dome of the cruiser sealed around me, I saw the rest of my flight scrambling to get into their own cruisers. For a minute, it was silent save for the rushing of blood in my ears.

I could help this time. No one else had to die.

I flipped the buttons to engage the start sequence. A light blinked on my comms—someone was requesting a chat over a private radio channel. I almost ignored it, but it was from Dragon Six.

Paige.

"What is it, Books?" Her call sign rolled off my tongue.

"Research Station Beta . . ." she trailed off. "Is that—"

"Yeah."

"Understood."

And that was that. She had my back.

"Alright, team," Amara's voice crackled over the flight radio. "Who's ready to save some nerds?"

There was a general whoop over the comms.

"Lift off and form up in flight order," Amara commanded. I rechecked my cruiser's readouts three times waiting for Dragons One through Four to lift off and hover out the open hangar door.

"Sky?" Paige's voice came over our still open private line. "Did you eat anything when we got back?"

"No, I got distracted working on the tech-bomb problem."

"Did you sleep?"

"Uh . . . some."

I could practically hear her rolling her eyes at me. "If you pass out and crash, I'm gonna kill you."

I couldn't respond. All I could think of was my parents. Had they been exploded by some bomb? Were they slowly suffocating, crushed by rubble? Somehow, Paige knew what I was thinking.

"Don't panic, Skylar. We'll get there in time."

The use of my real name pulled me back from my morbid brain spiral. I looked at the cruiser beside me. I could make out Paige's helmet in her cockpit, she was looking at me. I nodded my thanks to her, not trusting myself to speak.

Then it was my turn to lift off. I shot out of the hangar faster than regulations allowed, wingmate on my tail.

Three

P aige was born to fly. She shot down yet another of my tails
while I focused on the enemy in front of me.

Sure, I could hold my own in a battle. When I locked into
a firefight, I hyper-focused. Nothing could distract me. My
reflexes were quick and my aim was sharp. I practiced in the
cockpit as often as I could, but Paige could still fly circles around
me.

"Thanks, Books," I called down our private line.

"I've got your six, Sky. Keep after those hostile bombers."

We were learning how the aliens fought. Recently, they had
been sending a fleet of two or three bombers disguised within
their fighters. Those bombers were slower and bulkier, but
wreaked havoc if they got through our defenses. Not just in the
physical sense, but also to our technology.

A bomb had dropped on the Civ to the south of us and
knocked out their communications for a month. Even our
rescue fleet went dark when they passed through the bomb's

perimeter. Apparently, the bomb contained some sort of chemical that, while not immediately toxic to humans, shorted out all tech in range. The effects lasted long enough that we sent in a HazMat team to neutralize the substance. Eventually, they got it cleared up and the tech started working again.

Since then, I'd made a point of keeping watch for those bulky ships whenever we engaged the enemy. It was easy for me to spot their strange flight pattern. It was crucial we identified the bombers and blow them up far from their targets, above where the tech-bomb would be effective. If the Station was hit, countless experiments would be compromised, along with the facilities that grew most of our food.

Thousands would die.

"I've almost got this one." The bomber was leading me on a good chase, but I wouldn't let it out of my sight. "Are there any more?"

"Songbird and Buzz are pursuing the last one," Paige responded over the comms. "Tater and Caps are distracting the fighters. Need an assist?"

I fired my blaster and made a direct hit. The exploding ruins of the bomb was answer enough.

"Alright, then." Paige chuckled. "Guess not—shit."

"Books?"

"I flew too close, the bomb got my left engine." Her voice was strained. "I gotta glide down."

My heart was in my throat as Paige coasted toward the Station below. I followed her descent, wishing I could reach into her cockpit and pull her to safety. I covered her as she landed in the rarely-used hangar, then I returned to the fight.

I spun my cruiser around, looking for another enemy. Songbird and Buzz had just detonated the last bomber and the alien fighters were retreating.

"Songbird," Caps called through the comms. "Do we give chase?"

"Negative," Amara said. "Let them go. Form up. I'm requesting permission to land."

I relaxed in my cockpit as I maneuvered into my spot in the formation. Hovering there, my exhaustion finally caught up to me. I pulled off my helmet and rubbed my eyes with shaking hands. I did it—my parents were safe.

The Station far below looked so much smaller than it had ´ when I was a kid. Had it really been seven years since Si and I stole those bikes and rode through the greenhouse? It seemed like yesterday.

Dragon Flight descended, one by one, leaving me in the air. I blinked before comprehending. Right, my helmet. My flight couldn't speak to me without it. I slid my helmet back on to the sounds of radio chatter.

"I'm exhausted," Buzz said. "We're in no state to do PR."

"Hey," Tater responded, "I'll talk to anyone if there's food."

"Of course you will," Caps muttered.

"What's that supposed to mean, Caps?"

"You're *always* hungry."

"Whatever—"

We landed in a rusty hangar filled with plants. It was partially open to the outside where bits of the roof had fallen away. I hopped out of my cruiser and ran to where Paige stood waiting. I looked her over, but didn't see any obvious injuries.

"You scared me."

"I'm fine." She grimaced. "Can't say the same for my cruiser."

"We'll fix it."

We joined the rest of our flight as a man in a security uniform approached us. He had salt and pepper hair and walked with a bit of a hunch. My jaw dropped when I recognized Sheriff Larz. The slightly stooped, older man was a far cry from the Larz of my childhood. How had my perception of him changed so drastically? I looked around, half expecting my parents to rush through the hangar doors—but no. Why would they?

"Thank you, Captain." Larz saluted Amara, then the rest of us. "Our thanks to all of you for defending our citizens. I am Sheriff Jerald Larz. You are all welcome to—"

His gaze met mine and he paused. I flashed him a smile and I could have sworn tears glazed his eyes. Then he blinked and was all business again. There was the Larz I knew.

"—stay here for as long as you need. We invite you to tour our facility and sample our newly engineered crops."

Amara silenced Tater's whoop at the mention of food with a sharp look.

"Thank you, Sheriff." Amara smiled at Larz. "A meal and a place to bunk would be excellent. My team has been worn rather thin the last few days."

"Try the last few months," Caps muttered under her breath.

"Our home is your home." Larz gestured for us to follow him. "Right this way, I'll get you settled in. Though, I'm sure Airman Monahue could show you around. Nothing has changed since he left."

All eyes turned to me. Most were confused, but Amara's were angry. I had rushed us into this mission when we weren't at our full strength, and I didn't even tell her why. I had made a reckless decision and pulled the rest of them with me.

Well, that's why I wasn't flight leader.

I shrugged. Amara shook her head. Paige discreetly bumped her shoulder against mine to show her support.

Larz led us to the cafeteria. Caps ordered two cups of coffee and Tater almost broke into happy tears when she saw the small red potatoes on the menu. We had just finished eating when the voices around us hushed.

My whole body tensed at the sight of the woman standing frozen in the doorway. Her hand flew to her mouth and her hazel eyes widened. I scrambled to my feet, suddenly hyper aware of my limbs and unsure what to do with them. I tried for a casual smile, but I was pretty sure it looked as awkward as I felt. Seven years suddenly felt like a very long time.

"Hi, Mom."

Tears streamed down her cheeks and she ran to me, engulfing me in a hug. I squeezed her back, surprised at the sudden emotion in my chest. She was smaller than I remembered, but she smelled like home.

"You're safe?" She pulled back, holding my face between her palms.

"Yeah Mom, I'm safe."

She threw her arms around me again and wept. I shot a nervous glance at my flight, but their expressions ranged from adoring to wistful. Even Amara smiled.

"Go spend some time with your family, Sky," Amara said. "We'll be here a while."

I blinked at the unexpected order, but nodded. I shot Paige a pleading look. After a quick conversation with Amara, she followed us out of the cafeteria.

Four

I t was a weird collision of worlds, having Paige in the same room as my parents.

"This is Paige. She's my . . ." I looked down at Paige and she met my stare. I panicked. "Uh . . . wingmate."

I still wasn't sure what our relationship was. Ever since that first night she came to my room to vent, we'd grown close. We found little excuses to touch. A hand on the shoulder to show support. An arm around the other to lend strength. Sometimes a hug. We needed each other this past year. Though, neither of us had the courage to bring up the 'relationship' conversation.

That wasn't something I planned on approaching in front of my parents.

"We've missed you, Skylar." Mom blotted at her cheeks with a cloth. "Tell us what you've been doing."

Dad snorted. "We know what he's been doing, Connie. He's in the military; they only do one thing."

"Actually, I've been working with the engineers to—"

"Create better ways to kill, no doubt."

The words brought me up short. Was there any way to convince him I was working to protect people?

"No, I've been experimenting—"

"The only experiments the military does cost lives." Dad pointed to the decorations on my flight suit. "How many lives did you take to get those medals?"

What could I say? Telling him I single handedly shot down dozens of pilots wouldn't positively color his opinion of me, even though my actions saved hundreds of lives.

Dad looked Paige up and down. "Young lady, how much do you really know about your *wingmate*?"

I clenched my jaw and curled my fingers into fists.

"Isaac," Mom warned. He ignored her.

"Did he tell you about his brother?"

"Some." Paige looked at me, but I looked away. Of *course* he would bring up Silas.

"Did he tell you it was a fighter pilot from *your* military that dropped that bomb?"

I shook my head. "It wasn't—"

"Did he tell you he abandoned his mother and me without a word?"

"That's not—"

"Did he tell you that he brought his brother to an off-limits area right before his death?"

"I didn't—"

"If Silas hadn't been up there," Dad yelled, "he would have lived."

My arguments shriveled on my tongue and I rocked back on my heels. There wasn't a day that went by that I didn't blame myself for Silas' death. I assumed my parents blamed me too, but to hear him say it . . .

"We are scientists," Dad continued. "Silas wouldn't have wanted you to run away and join the *military*, of all things."

Silence fell over the room. The tension between us was combustible. It would only take five words from me to set it off. To light up the room like a firefight.

You didn't even know him.

But what was the point? Dad wouldn't listen to me anyway. Like always, I held my tongue. Without a word, I turned on my heel and strode from the room.

"Skylar, please!" Mom called after me, but I didn't stop. I couldn't talk to her right now, especially with *him* in the room. I would say something I would regret, and that'd be worse than not saying anything.

I was halfway down the plant-lined corridor when Paige caught up to me. She took my arm and pulled me to a stop, but I couldn't look at her. I closed my eyes and focused on taking long, slow breaths.

"Sky, you're shaking."

I pulled free of her grasp and slammed my fist into the concrete wall. And again. And again. The sharp pain across my knuckles focused me.

"I knew it would be like this," I forced through gritted teeth. "They don't see me—just the uniform. I just want to protect them, Paige."

"I know, Sky." Tentative fingers brushed my shoulder. When I didn't move, she pulled me to face her. "I see you. I see everything you've done. I'm proud of you."

I pulled her into a hug to hide the tears forming in my eyes.

"You're amazing," I whispered into her hair. "What did I do to deserve you?" I tensed when I realized I said the words aloud. I cleared my throat. "A-as a wingmate."

"Probably something reckless." Her words were muffled.

I laughed.

"Come on." She pulled away from me and inspected my bloody knuckles. "Show me where the med-bay is."

Five

I looked at my clock again. 0238. I hadn't slept at all, despite lying in bed for three hours. My patience was shot. I hated when my brain got in these ruts where it just wouldn't stop churning.

I couldn't get comfortable. My skin felt overly sensitive where the blanket pressed against it. I was too hot, then too cold. I tossed and turned, trying to find the perfect position that would let me fall into oblivion.

If I was in my room back at the barracks, I could work on my plethora of projects until my mind was focused enough to relax. Recently, I'd been trying to find a way to counteract the tech-bombs. I didn't have that option, here. I just had to lay in bed and replay my mother's pained expression. My father's disappointment at my life choices. My—

A quiet knock sounded at my door.

I shot out of bed, thankful for the distraction. I pulled open the door to find Paige. She had her arms crossed over the Station-issued pajamas—a loose beige shirt and matching trousers. We had flown out of our base so quickly, no one had time to pack a bag. Even in borrowed clothes two sizes too big, she was beautiful.

"Did I wake you?" Paige whispered.

"No." I opened the door wider. "Come in."

She flashed me a quick smile before sliding into my room. I yawned and closed the door behind her.

"Thanks, I . . ." She trailed off and glanced around the room.

"Books, what's wrong?"

"Nothing." She shifted her weight from one foot to the other and rubbed at her arms.

"Are you cold?"

"No, I'm just . . ." She huffed out a frustrated sigh and shook her head. "These plants are freaking me out. I can't sleep."

I glanced at the potted plants scattered around the room. "The plants?"

"Yes! I feel like they're going to tangle me up or smother me in my sleep."

I couldn't help it. I laughed.

She flushed and her shoulders hunched in the slightest amount. That quelled my amusement immediately.

"I'm sorry. I'm not laughing at you." I rushed to explain. "Silas used to say the same thing when we were kids."

She peered up at me. "Your brother?"

I nodded. "We shared a room, so he would always crawl into bed with me when he got scared."

"I'm not scared." Her voice was smaller than I'd ever heard it.

"Sleep with me, anyway."

Her eyebrows shot up and her cheeks tinged a pale pink. It took me a minute to understand why.

"No, not—sorry. I mean . . ." I ran my hand through my hair as my own cheeks heated. God, I was tired. "Just to sleep. We both need to sleep."

She relaxed a little and gave a nervous chuckle.

"Yeah, alright."

What was that tone? I tried not to read into it as we got into bed. We'd fallen asleep beside each other dozens of times in the last year, but not intentionally. Usually, she would come to my room to talk and we would drift off. Sliding under the covers beside her tonight had a significantly different feeling. We were stiff for a moment, until she sighed and rested her head on my shoulder, letting me wrap my arms around her.

She was so tough—so independent—but sometimes she would melt into me. It made me feel whole. Powerful. Like together, we could accomplish anything. It also gave my churning brain something to focus on. I ran my fingers up and down her bare arms, relishing in her warmth. How could something so strong feel so soft?

"What did you tell Silas?" Her breath on my skin gave me goosebumps. "To make him less scared of the plants."

"We would talk about why each plant was cultivated and what they do to help humanity."

"Yeah?"

"Like that one in the corner is a Citrus Perfume. It aerosolizes vitamin C, so we can breathe it in. Much easier than growing enough oranges to feed the Civs. That one—" I pointed to the Thymary, "—is great for cooking, and it's believed to be good for mental health. Plus it smells great. The fern here is one of my favorites. It's been around since the dinosaurs. It's hardy and good for air purification. I've actually been studying this one to see if I can genetically modify it to absorb whatever chemical is in those tech-bombs. Unfortunately, the vascular systems of terrestrial plants aren't made to absorb alien chemicals . . ."

I jolted up in bed, jostling Paige.

"Ouch," she grumbled.

"Sorry, are you okay?" I looked back and found her grinning.

"I was worried about the plants, but I should have been worried about you."

I slid out of bed and hurried to the panel on the wall to access the Station's current research. I gestured to the fern. "Alien chemicals. Paige, we need an *alien* plant."

"Do we . . . have one?"

I turned my attention back to the screen. "Possibly."

"You aren't going to sleep tonight, are you?" Paige joined me at the panel and read over my shoulder.

"Uh . . . maybe?"

"Do what you have to." She yawned. "Wake me if you discover something cool."

"Define 'cool.'" I smiled as she climbed back into my bed and curled up under the blankets.

"Breakthroughs, only."

"Got it."

Six

D r. Roe's lab was, somehow, both different and exactly the same. Unfamiliar technicians worked among the familiar, plant-covered lab benches. Dr. Roe may have died in the bombing, but his work persisted. Dr. Lucus, the new lead scientist, stared at me like I was crazy when I told him my plan. Luckily, my parents had come with me. Otherwise he probably would have tossed me in the compost bin.

"Look," I said, "Dr. Roe was attempting to genetically recombine terrestrial plants with the sample of alien flora we recovered. If we're lucky, he's already done the hard work for us and we'll just have to grow the thing."

"This lab was a mess when I started," Dr. Lucus said. "Nothing was labeled appropriately. I didn't even know we had alien flora."

"Dr. Roe had his own labeling conventions." I smiled at the memory of the kindly old man. His mess drove me crazy until I figured out his organization pattern. I gestured toward the row of freezers along the wall. "May I?"

"Be my guest."

He typed in his code so I could access the freezer's digital readout. I quickly scrolled through the labelled contents, looking for—there! ET01. The extraterrestrial samples. Now to find the recombined plants.

I scrolled through pages and pages of crosses. Dr. Roe had started several seeds—more than I expected—but ferns reproduce using spores. Hopefully, he made it to Polypodiophyta. I froze, fingers hovering over the screen.

ET01xPPD

That was it. It had to be.

I selected the sample and it ejected from the freezer slot with a hiss of cold air. I rushed to the lab bench and pulled on some gloves before popping open the freezer vial. Cryoliquid dumped into my palm, followed by a small, heart shaped gametophyte with a tiny prothallus protruding from the top. I grinned up at my parents.

Mom jumped to work, gathering the necessary supplies while dad came to look over my shoulder.

"See son?" Dad implored. "You could help people if you'd stayed here."

"I do help people, Dad."

"Silas would have wanted you to stay here, not—"

"You didn't even know him, did you?" I rounded on him. "I'm doing what he wanted to do. I'm living out *his* dream."

Dad's face grew red and I could tell he was about to explode, but Mom stepped up beside me, depositing the lab equipment on the bench.

"That's *enough*, Issac," she hissed. "Your anger will not cost me the only son I have left."

Dad stared between Mom and me for a few seconds, then turned and left.

I deflated. "I'm sorry, I shouldn't have—"

"You have nothing to be sorry for." Her eyes filled with tears. "You need to live your own life. Not the one we planned for you."

I didn't know what to say, so I reached for the pipette.

Paige burst through the door of the lab, Caps and Tater on her heels.

"Sky, there's been a transmission from Commander Shale. There's a fleet of combatants on their way here. Mostly bombers."

I stood from the lab bench, ignoring the stiffness in my back.

"Griffin and Phoenix Flights are en route," she continued, "but we have orders to stall the enemy until they arrive. You need to get up there."

I glanced back at the pot on the workbench. A single tech-bomb could wipe out this facility and we only had six—no, five—cruisers to fight them.

"You should go," I told Paige. "Take Dragon Five. You're the better pilot. I'm needed here."

She narrowed her eyes at the tiny plant. "Do you think it will work?"

I nodded.

"Okay, then."

I pulled her into a hug. "Be careful."

"Be quick." She pulled back just enough to look at me. "We aren't going to be able to stop all of them. This experiment may be the human race's only hope."

"So no pressure."

She smirked. "If anyone can do it, it's you, Sky."

"Seriously, Paige, no unnecessary risks." She blinked at my use of her name, rather than her callsign. I lowered my voice. "Not while I'm not up there with you."

"Don't worry, Sky," Caps cut in. "She'll be with Tater and me. We'll watch her six. You can trust us."

"It's not you two I'm worried about," I growled.

I hadn't lifted my gaze from Paige's face. Her mouth softened and, for some reason, she blushed. I tried to memorize the way her blue eyes shimmered in the fluorescent grow lights, the excited flush of her cheeks, and the pale pink of her upturned lips.

"I'll be okay, Skylar." She stood on her toes and placed a kiss on my cheek. I was suddenly very warm. "I promise."

I tightened my grip on her. It took me a moment to respond, and when I did, my voice was rough.

"I'll hold you to that."

I was close enough to see her pupils dilate.

"Wanna listen?" She pulled an earpiece from her pocket.

I nodded and she slipped it over my ear.

"Good." She stepped back and I let my arms fall to my sides. "I'll see you soon."

"I'll see you soon."

Paige opened her mouth to say something else, then shut it again.

"Come on, Books." Tater said from where she and Caps were waiting by the door. "Songbird is calling."

Paige nodded. Her expression hardened as it always did when she prepared for a firefight. Without another word, she turned and left. Minutes later, I heard the familiar sounds of liftoff in my ear. I could hear the flight chatter and their conversation with Ground Command. It felt weird when Dragon Five was called, but it wasn't me in the cockpit.

I focused on my work with Mom at the lab bench. We used some super-growth serum concoction to speed the growth of the prothallus and a concentrated purple laser to mature the fern.

"This is amazing," I said, watching the fronds grow under the laser beam.

Mom smiled. "We've come a long way in the last few years. Conferring with the other Stations has progressed us further than we thought possible."

I kept one ear on the chatter as I worked. My team was in the thick of battle, but Griffin and Phoenix Flights were close. They just had to hold out until—

"So, when are you going to tell that girl you love her?"

I dropped the laser.

"*Mom.*" Heat flooded my face.

"What? She obviously cares for you, too."

"Now is *not* the time."

"I'm just saying." Mom shrugged. "Tomorrow is never guaranteed. Especially in your line of work." Mom switched off her light. "This is ready. Let's get it outside."

I grabbed the fern and sprinted to the stairwell, Mom on my heels. I started down, but Mom halted me.

"No, this way!" She started up the steps toward the roof.

I swallowed, but followed her, taking the steps two at a time. Younger and fitter, I quickly passed her. I shouldered open the door to the rooftop greenhouse and froze. It had been repaired since the bomb and looked just as I remembered it—down to the row of bikes lined up beside the door. Like the bomb never hit. Like Silas never died.

Like I never failed.

"Skylar?" Mom had caught up while I stood frozen.

"I haven't been here since . . ."

Mom put her hand on my shoulder. I don't know how long I stood there, but the voice in my earpiece brought me back to myself.

"*Shit, I've got another tail.*" Paige's voice crackled over my earpiece. "*Caps, where are you? I can't shake it.*"

"*I was hit.*" Caps sounded like she was crying. "*I have no control—have to eject!*"

"*Tater?*" Paige shouted. No response.

"*I've got you, Books.*" That was Tristan from Griffin Flight. Never thought I'd be happy to hear his voice.

Paige's sigh of relief told me she was safe—for the moment.

"*Thanks, Twist.*"

"*Where's Sky?*" Tristan asked.

"*He's busy saving our lives.*" Her absolute faith in me took my breath away. "*Wanna team up?*"

"*Just like old times.*"

I'd punch him if he survived the battle. Or maybe hug him. Both seemed plausible.

Alarms blared in the greenhouse, drowning out their voices. I forced my thoughts back to my task, relaxing my fingers from their white-knuckled grip. Paige was safe—for now—but for how long?

I turned to Mom. "Let's go."

It was a strange sensation, running deeper into the trails beneath the screaming alarm. It was the opposite of my sprint with Silas. I was older and had more training, but was just as terrified as I had been that night. There was more riding on this battle—more to lose.

It wasn't just my friends and family that could die, but entire Civs. Maybe my entire species. If this didn't work and the aliens discovered how much destroying a Research Station hurt us, humanity wouldn't last the year.

"There!" Mom pointed at a door and I barreled through it onto a small balcony.

Dry heat hit me and I coughed through my gasps. The door swung shut behind us, cutting off the screaming alarm. Amara's distressed voice crackled through my ear.

"—*respond, Books, I repeat: please respond*!"

I watched in horror as Dragon Five took a nosedive. An unresponsive pilot couldn't pull the eject lever.

"Eject!" I screamed, knowing she couldn't hear me. Once again, I was helpless. "Paige, eject—"

A tech-bomb exploded above me. The force pushed me back against the wall and the fern fell from my hands. Humanity's last hope smashed to the ground in a pile of topsoil. My stomach dropped—I failed. I couldn't protect anyone. Not my brother. Not Paige. Not my parents. Not this world.

The fern exploded with growth. Branches burst from the soil, growing longer and thicker than physically possible. They weren't typical fern leaves but had thick branches with long spindly leaves protruding from the vines—similar to the antennae of a moth. They twisted and tangled into the sky, reaching toward where the bomb went off like the roots of a desert plant reach for water.

The plant didn't stop. New growth sprouted from the fronds and continued to grow up into the sky, through the battling cruisers. It wove through where bombs previously detonated, tangling up and immobilizing the aircraft. Within seconds, visibility was abysmal and the battle went still.

"It must be reacting to the chemical in the bombs." Mom pulled me into a hug. "Skylar, you did it!"

I held her close, looking around desperately, trying to see through the vines as the strong, feathery fronds swayed in the dry wind. I strained my sound-damaged ears to listen to the quiet voice in my earpiece.

"*Sound off, Dragon Flight!*" Amara ordered over the coms. I held my breath as Dragons One through Four reported in.

"*Dragon Five here.*" Paige's voice was weak and scratchy, but it was the most beautiful thing I'd ever heard. I would have fallen over had Mom not been holding me. "*This plant tried to smother me, but it caught me before I hit the ground. Sky, if you're listening down there—great work. I knew you could do it."*

"She's safe." I laughed and buried my head into my mom's shoulder. A weight lifted from my shoulders. I *wasn't* useless anymore. I *could* protect the people I loved. "They're all safe. We did it."

"*You* did it, Skylar." Mom squeezed me tighter. "What should we name this life-saving creation?"

That was easy. "Silas."

We were alone on the roof, but I could have sworn a second set of arms wrapped around me.

Seven

It was hours before we could recover the pilots from their crafts. After the initial shock, every capable body in the Station banded together to help the brave soldiers who saved their home. The attitude was a far cry from the anti-military sentiment I grew up with.

Teams worked in rotating shifts, climbing and cutting vines to open the cruiser cockpits. We were required to rest thirty minutes for every two hours we worked to prevent the crews from getting tired and making deadly mistakes. I was honestly surprised the scientists didn't stop to write out a proposal prior to starting the rescue, but a few sharp words from Larz got them going.

I was in my rest rotation, preparing to go back out early when Mom found me. I had worked through my first few breaks, but Larz had noticed and forced me to come grab a meal.

Mom smiled. "They finally got Paige down."

I fumbled with the ration bar I'd been attempting to scarf down.

"Where?"

"Med-bay six!"

I was already running.

I slammed open the door to the medical bay and skidded to a stop at row six.

"Paige?" I pressed through the closed curtain and froze.

Her flight suit was pulled down to her hips, leaving her in a standard white sleeveless undershirt. She grimaced as the doctor pulled down her shoulder strap to inspect the bruising there. The deep blue mark continued across her chest and disappeared beneath her shirt. Another marred the opposite shoulder, crossing the first in the shadow of our cruiser restraints.

"I'm okay." Paige's face transformed as she smiled up at me.

My stomach flipped like I was executing an upward loop at the relief that shot through me. Before I could speak, the doctor shot me a glare.

"Just because you saved the Station, Mr. Monahue," the doctor said, "doesn't mean you get to barge into my med-bay."

"S-sorry." I backed away as reality snapped into place. Heat flooded my face. I had seen Paige in less clothing, but somehow this seemed more invasive. "I didn't mean to—"

"Wait, Sky." She turned to the doctor. "He can stay."

"Fine." He carefully replaced her strap and lifted the hem of her undershirt to probe deft fingers across her ribs.

She sucked in a sharp breath when he reached her left side. I jolted forward and took her hand in mine. She squeezed my fingers.

"Looks like a fractured rib." He pulled her shirt back down and quickly checked each of her legs, flexing every joint. "Any other pain?"

Paige shook her head.

"Good. I'll get the nurses to bring you something for the pain, but there's not much we can do for this type of injury." He wrote some notes on a chart, then looked at me. "Make sure she takes it easy for the next few days."

I laughed—like I had any control over what she did.

"I'm serious. No flying for at least a week. She was hanging from those restraints for hours. If she goes back up, it will not only hurt like hell, it will risk further injury. No flying. No exercise." He glanced between us. "No sex."

My face burned. "No, we—we aren't . . . I mean . . ."

"Don't care." The doctor peeled off his gloves and tossed them in a bin on his way through the curtain. "I've got work to do."

Paige's laughter pulled my attention from the curtain swishing closed behind him.

"Ouch," she clutched at her side, still chuckling.

"Are you—"

"I'm fine, Sky." She didn't let go of my hand. "You did it."

"Barely." I placed a palm to her cheek and she leaned into me, eyes half closing. "I almost lost you."

"I'm not going anywhere."

"I . . ."

I leaned closer. Paige's eyes widened, but she didn't lean away. I was close enough to see her pupils dilate.

Interest, or brain injury? a far-off part of my brain asked.

I froze. What was I doing? She just had a near death experience. She could have a concussion or be on some sort of medication that impaired her judgement. Now was *not* the time to make a move. I could wait.

I pulled away. Before I could get far, Paige grabbed the collar of my flight suit, capturing me without any difficulty. Time stretched around us as we stared at each other. Electricity buzzed through me when her gaze dropped to my lips. Then, slowly—so slowly—Paige leaned toward me.

My breath caught when her lips pressed into mine. The rest of the world fell away. Air, water, sunlight—it was just her. It had always been her. I ran my fingers through her silky hair. I wanted to pull her close—to pick her up and hold her against me—but I refrained. I kissed her so carefully, my hands shook with the effort of my restraint.

Still, Paige flinched and a whine escaped her lips. I pulled back immediately.

"Sorry," I gasped. "Did I hurt you?"

"No." She grimaced. "It's my ribs. I guess the doctor was right about . . ." She cleared her throat and her cheeks flushed pink. "I can't believe I ruined our first kiss with my stupid injury."

"You didn't ruin anything. You couldn't. You're perfect."

I helped her lean back on the cot and smoothed a stray lock of hair behind her ear. She looked exhausted, but I probably wasn't much better. I looked around for somewhere to sit, but there was nothing in the small space. I was about to go look for a chair to pull up to her bed, but she squeezed my fingers tighter.

"Don't leave." Her voice was so small, I couldn't respond. "Please."

I eased onto the cot beside her and carefully wrapped an arm around her. She let out a sigh and closed her eyes, snuggling into me.

"Don't worry Paige. I'm not going anywhere."

About the Author

L eah Lore is a fantasy and science fiction author from southwest Ohio. An avid reader from a young age, she was constantly daydreaming stories to escape reality. When not writing, Leah can be found at the stable with her unicorn, hiking in the woods with her partner and their rescue dog, or under a fluffy blanket with her cats and a good book.

Leah was a finalist in the 2024 NYCMidnight Short Story Challenge and her short stories have been published in several anthologies. Leah's debut full-length novel, a new-adult portal fantasy, will hit the shelves in fall 2025.

Leah's stories are character-driven adventures with an emphasis on mental health and self-worth. She has an MS in biology from Wright State University. Her education and love of nature have been pivotal elements of creating beautiful yet realistic worlds brimming with magic.

If you enjoyed this story, please leave a review! Follow Leah's progress on her website and social media by scanning the QR code below.

https://linktr.ee/leahlore

Acknowledgements

I have so many people to thank for this project. First and foremost, I want to thank Rochelle Bradley for mentoring me on all things book related, dragging me to book conventions, and introducing me to some of the best people—not to mention answering my unhinged publishing questions at all hours of the day.

I also want to thank Sara Copes for going above and beyond in designing my cover and chapter images. I'll never look at this book on the shelf without craving pineapple fried rice and brown sugar milk tea.

A huge thanks to my many editors and beta readers for making this world sparkle, and to my friends and family for your unending support. I can't tell you how much I appreciate you. May you all reach the stars.